My Sound Box

by Jane Belk Moncure
illustrated by Pam Peltier

THE CHILD'S WORLD

MANKATO, MN 56001

Library of Congress Cataloging in Publication Data

Moncure, Jane Belk.
   My "u" sound box.

   (Sound box books)
   Summary: The umbrellas Little u keeps in her sound
box prove very useful to her uncle, an umpire, and others,
when it begins to rain.
   1. Children's stories, American.   [1. Alphabet]
I. Peltier, Pam, ill.   II. Title.   III. Series.
PZ7.M739Myu 1984   [E]   84-17012
ISBN 0-89565-300-1 -1991 Edition

My "u" Sound Box

(This book uses only the short "u" sound in the story line. Words beginning with the long "u" sound are included at the end of the book.)

Little  had a

"I will find things that begin with my 'u' sound," she said.

"I will put them into my sound  box.

First, I will find an umbrella.

I will run, run, run

to find an umbrella.''

Why did Little  get under the box?

Why was the box upside down?

Little found an umbrella.

She found lots of umbrellas.

She put one umbrella over her head.
Did she put the other umbrellas

into her box?

She did.

Just then the sun came out.

Little put the umbrella down.

But then the rain came down again.

Little   put the umbrella
up.

Then she saw some underclothes.

They were getting wet.

She took the underclothes off the line.

She put them into her box.

Little  took the underclothes upstairs.

She put the underclothes away.

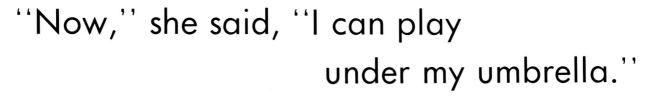

"Now," she said, "I can play
under my umbrella."

She went out in the rain.

"I can run through a

mud puddle,"

she said. "What fun!"

Then Little  found an ugly duckling.

The ugly duckling was grumpy.

She put the ugly duckling into her box.

"Do not be grumpy," she said. "You will grow up to be beautiful."

Just then her uncle came by.

He was getting wet, so

Little ⊔ gave her uncle an umbrella.

Next, an umpire came by.

"Can you help us?" he said.

"We are playing baseball in the rain.
We need umbrellas."

Little  said, "I have a box full
of umbrellas."

She gave the umpire an umbrella.

Then she gave everyone an umbrella.

ugly
duckling

underclothes

umbrella

uncle

umpire

What fun they had in the rain.

Can you read these words with Little ?

undershirt

Uncle Sam

usher

umbrella bird

umbrella tree

29

Little  has another sound in some words.
She says her name, "u."

Can you read these words?
Listen for Little 's name.

ukulele

uniform

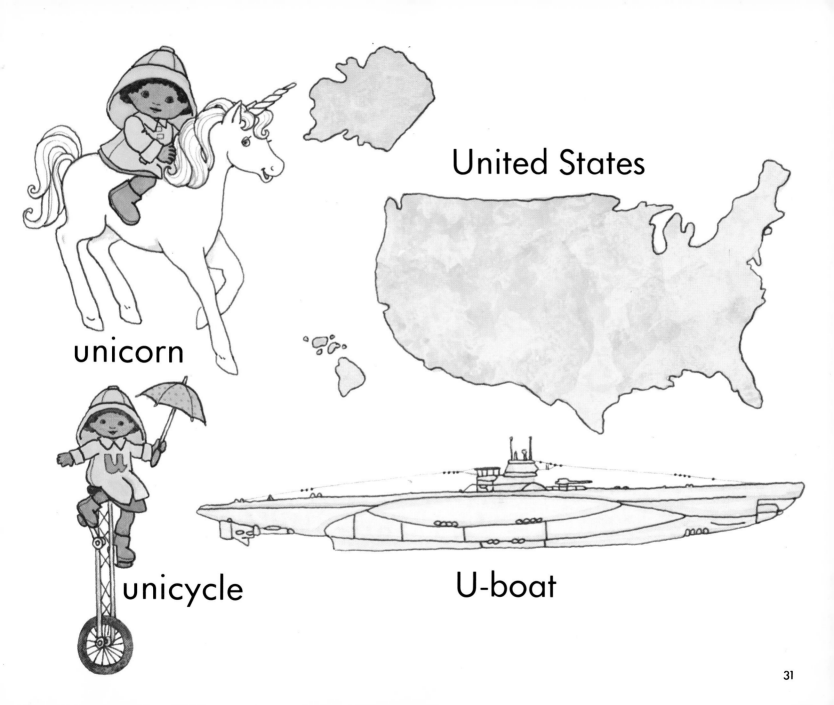

unicorn

United States

unicycle

U-boat

About the Author

Jane Belk Moncure began her writing career when she was in kindergarten. She has never stopped writing. Many of her children's stories and poems have been published, to the delight of young readers, including her son Jim, whose childhood experiences found their way into many of her books.

Mrs. Moncure's writing is based upon an active career in early childhood education. A recipient of an M.A. degree from Columbia University, Mrs. Moncure has taught and directed nursery, kindergarten, and primary grade programs in California, New York, Virginia, and North Carolina. As a member of the faculties of Virginia Commonwealth University and the University of Richmond, she taught prospective teachers in early childhood education.

Mrs. Moncure has traveled extensively abroad, studying early childhood programs in the United Kingdom, The Netherlands, and Switzerland. She was the first president of the Virginia Association for Early Childhood Education and received its award for oustanding service to young children.

A resident of North Carolina, Mrs. Moncure is currently a full-time writer and educational consultant. She is married to Dr. James A. Moncure, former vice president of Elon College.